For Michael, Andrew, and Tommy,
with love and adventure always.—M.M.

Illustrations copyright © 2016 by Mati McDonough
Book design by Sara Gillingham Studio

Printed in China

Library of Congress Control Number available
ISBN: 978-1-937359-83-6

10 9 8 7 6 5 4 3 2 1

cameron kids is an imprint of
Cameron + Company
6 Petaluma Blvd. North, Suite B-6
Petaluma, California 94952
www.cameronbooks.com

HOW DO I LOVE THEE?

by Elizabeth Barrett Browning

illustrated by Mati McDonough

cameron kids

How do I love thee?

Let me count the ways.

I love thee to the depth

and breadth and height

My soul can reach,

when feeling out of sight

For the ends of being and ideal grace.

I love thee to the level of every day's

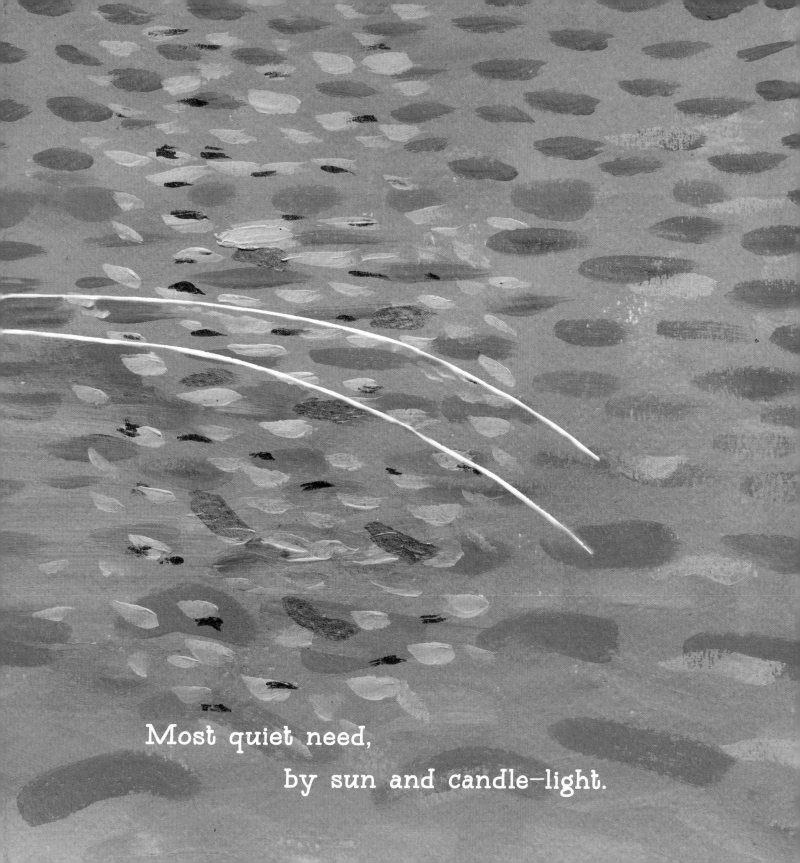

Most quiet need,
        by sun and candle-light.

I love thee freely, as men strive for right.

I love thee purely,
     as they turn from praise.

I love thee with the passion put to use

In my old griefs,
    and with my childhood's faith.

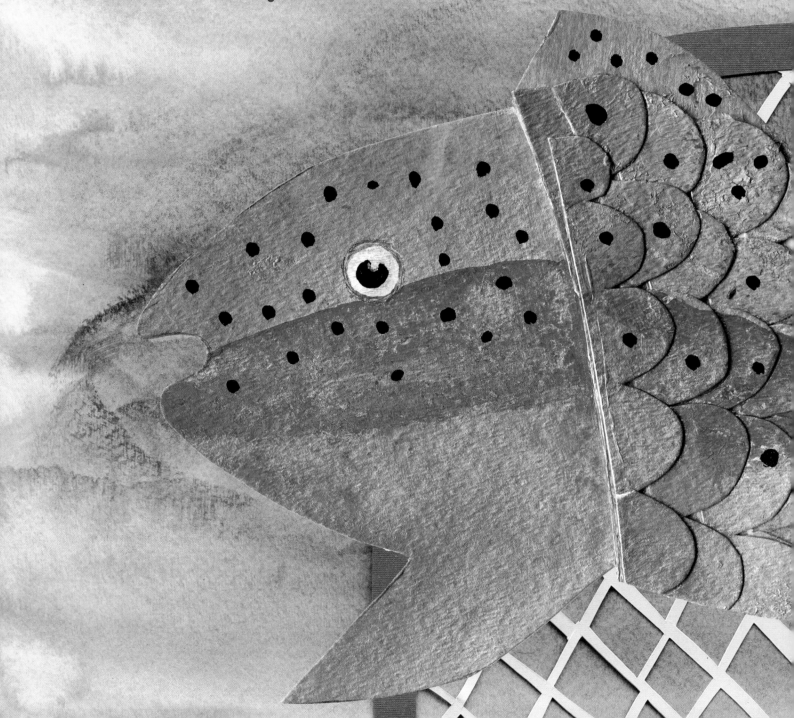

With my lost saints.

I love thee with the breath,
Smiles, tears, of all my life;

And, if God choose,

I shall but love thee better after death.